FOR MY BIG BROTHER DAVID,
WHO LIKED DOING UNRABBITY THINGS TOO X

First published in 2012 by Child's Play (International) Ltd
Ashworth Road, Bridgemead, Swindon SN5 7YD UK

Distributed in USA by Child's Play Inc
250 Minot Avenue, Auburn, Maine 04210

Distributed in Australia by Child's Play Australia Pty Ltd
Unit 10/20 Narabang Way, Belrose, NSW 2085

Text and illustrations copyright © 2012 Jo Empson
The moral right of the author/illustrator has been asserted

ISBN 978-1-84643-482-2
L251111CPL01124822

Printed and bound in Heshan, China

1 3 5 7 9 10 8 6 4 2

A catalogue record of this book is available from the British Library

www.childs-play.com

Rabbityness

By Jo Empson

Rabbit liked doing
rabbity things.

Rabbit liked hopping.

Rabbit liked jumping.

Rabbit liked twirling his whiskers.

Rabbit liked washing his ears.

Rabbit liked burrowing.

and Rabbit liked sleeping.

Rabbit also liked doing
unrabbity things.

...and making music.

This made Rabbit

VERY
happy!

It made him SO happy,
all the other rabbits caught his happiness.
He filled the woods with colour and music.

One day, Rabbit disappeared.

The other rabbits were very sad.
They couldn't find him anywhere.

The woods were quiet and grey.

All that Rabbit had left was a hole...

a

DEEP

dark

hole

But, down the DEEP, dark hole...

...Rabbit had left them some gifts.

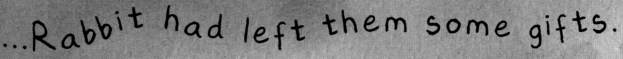

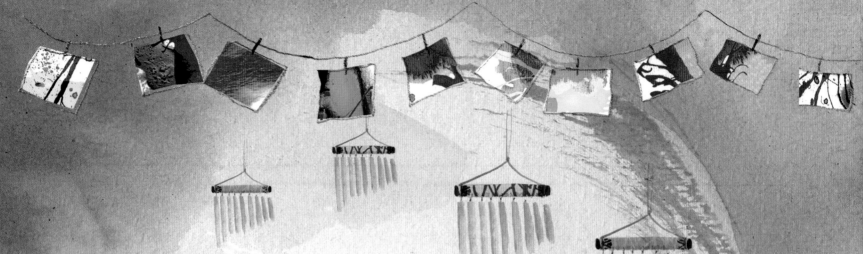

There were lots of things
to make colour and music.

chime
chime
chime
chime
chime
chime
chime

In time, all the rabbits discovered they liked doing unrabbity things too!

clang
clang

drum
drum
drum
drum
drum
drum

This made them think of Rabbit, which made them happy.

In fact, this made them SO happy...

...they filled the woods with colour and music once again!